GIRLS ARE AMAZING

Inspirational and Exciting Short Stories for Girls about Love, Self-Awareness and Courage | A Motivational Book for Young Girls I Gift for Girls

Linda Erickson

ISBN: 9798862762402

Table of Contents

Mirror, Mirror..5

Emma's Diary.. 11

The Talent Show... 17

Magical Garden.. 23

Harper's Goalkeeping Challenge 29

Max the Bully.. 36

Lisa's Heart Locket 42

The Secret Treasure Chest 49

The Lost Necklace.. 54

Jemma's Determination................................... 59

The Neighborhood Dragon............................... 66

Skating is For Girls 74

Messages on the Sidewalk 81

Searching for Seashells 89

The Art of Giving... 95

Mirror, Mirror

In a cozy little town, there lived a young girl named Lily. Lily's world was filled with wonder and curiosity. She loved exploring every nook and cranny of her house, and one sunny day, she decided to venture up into the dusty attic.

As she climbed the creaky stairs, she noticed a large, dusty mirror hidden behind a pile of old books and boxes. Lily wiped away the dust with her small hand and revealed a beautiful mirror with an ornate golden frame.

"Wow! This mirror is so pretty," Lily exclaimed, her eyes wide with amazement. She touched the mirror, and to her surprise, it began to shimmer and glow. She took a step back, but her curiosity got the best of her, and she peered into the mirror.

To her astonishment, she saw a girl who looked just like her, but a bit older. The girl in the mirror had sparkling eyes and a warm smile. "Hello there, Lily," the girl in the mirror said.

Lily gasped, her heart pounding with excitement. "Who are you?" she asked.

"I'm you, Lily, but I'm your future self," the girl in the mirror replied.

Lily couldn't believe her eyes. "Really? That's amazing! Can we talk?"

"Of course, we can," her future self said. "I'm here to help you learn some important things."

Over the next few days, Lily visited the magical mirror in the attic regularly. Each time, she talked to her future self, who shared stories and wisdom. They talked about adventures, dreams, and most importantly, they talked about self-love.

One day, as Lily looked into the mirror, she asked, "Why do you always look so happy, future me?"

Future Lily smiled warmly. "I'm happy because I've learned to love myself, just the way I am. You see, Lily, everyone is unique and special in their own way. Embracing what makes you different is the key to happiness."

Lily furrowed her little brow, trying to understand. "But what makes me special?"

Her future self replied, "You have a kind heart, Lily. You care about your friends and family, and you have a wonderful imagination. These are the things that make you special."

Lily nodded, beginning to grasp the concept of self-love. "So, I should love myself because of who I am inside?"

"That's right," her future self confirmed. "When you love yourself, you can love others even more. You can be confident and brave, just like the heroes in your favorite stories."

Lily felt a warm, fuzzy feeling inside her heart. She smiled and said, "I want to be like you when I grow up, future me."

Future Lily chuckled. "You don't have to wait to grow up to be like me, Lily. You can start loving yourself and embracing your uniqueness right now."

Inspired by her future self's words, Lily started to see herself in a new light. She realized that she didn't have to be like anyone else to be amazing. She could be herself, and that was enough.

As days turned into weeks, Lily's confidence grew. She no longer worried about what others thought of her. She embraced her love for painting, even if her artwork didn't always look perfect. She danced to her own tune, even if it made others laugh. She was simply Lily, and that was the most beautiful thing in the world.

One sunny afternoon, Lily looked into the magical mirror and said, "Thank you, future me. I feel so much happier and more confident now."

Future Lily smiled proudly. "You've learned a valuable lesson, Lily. Remember, the most important person to love is yourself. And always be kind, not only to others but to yourself as well."

Lily nodded, her eyes filled with determination. "I promise I will, future me. And I'll remind all my friends to love themselves too."

Time passed, and Lily continued to grow, both in wisdom and in her understanding of self-love. She shared the magic of the mirror with her friends, and they too learned the importance of self-love and embracing their unique qualities.

And so, in that cozy little town, the magical mirror in the attic became a symbol of self-acceptance and love. It taught generations of children that they were special just the way they were, and that their future selves would always be there to guide them with love and wisdom.

And as for Lily, she grew up to be a happy, confident, and kind-hearted young woman, just like her future self had shown her. She knew that the real magic wasn't in the mirror but in the love she had for herself and for others. And she carried that love with her, making her world a brighter and more beautiful place.

Emma's Diary

In a small town, nestled between rolling hills and a winding river, lived a curious and adventurous girl named Emma.

Emma had a heart full of dreams and a mind that thirsted for knowledge. She loved exploring the forest, chasing butterflies, and reading stories about far-off lands.

One sunny day, while exploring the attic of her family's old farmhouse, Emma stumbled upon an old leather-bound diary. Its pages were blank, but the diary felt warm and inviting in her hands. Emma opened it and, to her amazement, words began to appear on the pages as if by magic.

"Hello, Emma," the diary wrote in elegant script.

Emma's eyes widened with astonishment. "Hello?" she whispered, not quite sure if she was dreaming.

The diary replied, "I am the Diary of Infinite Possibilities. I am here to help you discover your strengths and weaknesses, and to teach you valuable life skills."

Emma's heart raced with excitement. "That sounds amazing! How do you work?"

The diary explained, "Each day, you can write about your experiences, thoughts, and feelings. I will respond with guidance and insights to help you grow."

From that day forward, Emma and the Diary of Infinite Possibilities became inseparable companions. Emma poured her heart and soul into the diary's pages, and it responded with wisdom and encouragement.

One morning, as Emma sat under her favorite oak tree, she wrote about her fear of speaking in front of her classmates. The diary replied, "Emma, the first step to conquering your fear is to believe in yourself. Remember, you have a voice worth hearing, and your words can inspire others."

With the diary's guidance, Emma practiced speaking in front of her stuffed animals, then in front of her family. Slowly but surely, her fear began to fade. She gained confidence in her abilities and soon found herself volunteering to give presentations at school.

Another time, Emma wrote about her struggles with patience. She often grew frustrated when things didn't go her way. The diary replied, "Patience is a valuable skill, Emma. Life doesn't always follow our plans. Embrace each moment, and you'll find joy in the journey."

Emma took the diary's advice to heart. She practiced patience by tending to her garden, watching the plants grow at their own pace. She learned to appreciate the beauty of waiting and discovered that life's sweetest moments often unfolded in unexpected ways.

As the days turned into weeks and the weeks into months, Emma's relationship with the diary deepened. It became her confidant, her mentor, and her source of inspiration.

Together, they explored the world of books, delving into tales of courage, kindness, and adventure. They shared dreams of far-off lands and daring quests.

One evening, Emma wrote about her dream of becoming a writer. She expressed her doubts and fears, wondering if her stories were good enough. The diary replied, "Emma, never doubt the power of your words. Your stories are unique, just like you. Share them with the world, and you'll touch hearts and minds."

With the diary's encouragement, Emma began to write stories from her heart. She poured her imagination onto the pages, creating characters and worlds that came alive with each word. She submitted her stories to a local writing contest and was overjoyed when she won first place. Her dream of becoming a writer felt closer than ever.

But it wasn't all about conquering fears and chasing dreams. The diary also helped Emma navigate the challenges of friendship and empathy. When she had disagreements with her friends, she wrote about her feelings of anger and hurt. The diary reminded her to listen with an open heart, to understand her friends' perspectives, and to forgive.

Through the diary's guidance, Emma learned the power of empathy and compassion. She mended her friendships and became a pillar of support for those around her. Her kindness and understanding were like a warm embrace to everyone she met.

One winter day, as Emma sat by the fireplace, she wrote in the diary about her gratitude for all the lessons it had taught her. The diary replied, "Emma, you have grown into a remarkable young person. Always remember that the journey of self-discovery is never-ending. Keep writing your story with courage and curiosity."

And so, Emma continued to write in the Diary of Infinite Possibilities, not just to seek guidance but also to record the beautiful moments of her life. She shared her triumphs, her setbacks, and her dreams. With each entry, she discovered more about herself and the world around her.

As the years passed, Emma's bond with the diary remained unbreakable. It was a testament to the power of self-reflection, guidance, and the belief that anything is possible when you have the courage to dream and the wisdom to learn from life's experiences.

And so, in that small town by the river, a girl named Emma found a trea sure that would stay with her for a lifetime—the Diary of Infinite Possibilities, a magical companion that guided her on a journey of self-discovery, wisdom, and endless wonder.

16

The Talent Show

In a peaceful little town nestled amidst lush green fields, there lived a quiet and thoughtful girl named Mia.

Mia was known for her gentle nature and her love for books. She found solace in the world of words, where characters from far-off lands became her friends, and adventures unfolded between the pages of her favorite novels.

While Mia cherished the company of her books and the tranquility of her thoughts, there was one thing she kept hidden from the world – a hidden treasure that even she was not aware of. Deep within her, Mia possessed a powerful and enchanting singing voice.

One sunny afternoon, as Mia was reading beneath her favorite tree, a gentle breeze rustling the pages of her book, her grandmother, a wise and observant woman, approached her.

"Mia," her grandmother said, her eyes twinkling with a secret, "have you ever sung for the trees?"

Mia blinked, surprised by the question. "No, Grandma. Why would I do that?"

Her grandmother smiled knowingly. "You have a voice, my dear, a voice that can bring joy to the world. It's time for you to discover it."

Mia was intrigued but also uncertain. She had always been the quiet girl in the background, content to let others take the spotlight. The idea of singing in front of people filled her with a strange mix of excitement and anxiety.

Weeks passed, and Mia's grandmother gently encouraged her to explore her singing talent. Late at night, when the world was asleep, Mia would tiptoe to the garden and sing softly to the moon and stars. Her voice was like a lullaby, soothing and tender.

One evening, as Mia sang to the moon, a passerby heard her melodic voice and stopped to listen. It was her music teacher, Mrs. Johnson. Impressed by Mia's voice, Mrs. Johnson approached her and offered to give her singing lessons.

Mia hesitated at first, her shyness holding her back, but her grandmother's words echoed in her mind. She agreed to the lessons, and under Mrs. Johnson's guidance, she began to discover the true potential of her singing voice.

With each lesson, Mia's voice grew stronger and more enchanting. She sang with a passion that came from deep within her soul. But as her talent blossomed, so did her self-doubt. The thought of singing in front of an audience filled her with a paralyzing fear.

One day, Mia's teacher announced that the school was hosting a talent show, and she encouraged Mia to participate. Mia's heart raced at the idea. The thought of standing on a stage in front of her classmates, teachers, and parents was terrifying.

As the days passed, Mia faced a dilemma. Should she share her gift with the world and conquer her fear, or should she keep it hidden, safe within the confines of her garden and moonlit nights?

One evening, Mia confided in her grandmother about her fear and uncertainty. Her grandmother smiled gently and said, "My dear, sometimes the most beautiful flowers bloom in the quietest corners of the garden. Your voice is a gift, and it deserves to be heard."

Encouraged by her grandmother's wisdom, Mia decided to take a leap of faith. She began to practice for the talent show, rehearsing her songs tirelessly with Mrs. Johnson. It wasn't easy; stage fright gnawed at her, and self-doubt whispered in her ear. But Mia was determined to overcome her fears.

As the day of the talent show drew nearer, Mia's nervousness reached its peak. She couldn't sleep, and she felt her stomach tie itself into knots. On the day of the show, her hands trembled as she stood backstage, waiting for her turn.

As the curtains opened and the spotlight fell upon her, Mia took a deep breath. She closed her eyes for a moment, visualizing her beloved garden and the moonlit nights. And then, she began to sing.

Her voice, once a whisper in the garden, now filled the auditorium with its beauty and power. As she sang, Mia felt a transformation within herself. Her fear melted away, replaced by the pure joy of sharing her gift with the world.

The audience was captivated by her voice, and a hush fell over the auditorium. Mia's song touched their hearts, and tears welled up in many eyes. When she finished, the applause was thunderous.

Mia had not only conquered her stage fright but had also discovered her own strength and the beauty of her talent. She had transformed from the quiet girl in the background into a confident and courageous young woman.

After the talent show, Mia continued to share her gift with the world. She sang at school events, in local community gatherings, and even in the town's annual music festival. Her voice became a source of inspiration, reminding everyone that hidden talents could blossom with courage and determination.

And so, in that peaceful little town, Mia's story became a testament to the power of self-discovery and the magic that can happen when one finds the courage to step onto the stage, face their fears, and let their unique talents shine.

22

Magical Garden

23

Two inseparable best friends named Emma and Sophia had a friendship that felt like sunshine on a cloudy day, warm and comforting. They did everything together, from exploring the woods to picking wildflowers, and even sharing secrets under their favorite oak tree.

One sunny morning, their sense of adventure led them deeper into the forest than they had ever ventured before. Birds chirped overhead, and a gentle breeze whispered through the leaves as Emma and Sophia wandered deeper into the woods. It was on this remarkable day that their lives would change forever.

As they ventured further, they stumbled upon an enchanting garden hidden behind a tangled thicket of vines and bushes. The garden was unlike anything they had ever seen, with flowers of every color, trees that seemed to whisper secrets, and a shimmering pond that sparkled like a thousand diamonds.

But what made this garden truly special was its magical ability to grant wishes. If you closed your eyes and made a heartfelt wish, the garden would listen, and somehow, those wishes would come true.

Emma and Sophia couldn't believe their luck. They each closed their eyes and made a wish. Emma wished for a rainbow-colored butterfly to land on her finger, and Sophia wished for the sweetest strawberries to appear by the pond. To their amazement, both wishes came true right before their eyes.

Excitement filled the air as they explored the garden further, making more wishes and watching them come to life. They wished for rainbows, bubbles, and even a playful squirrel to join them on their adventure.

As the day turned to evening, Emma and Sophia sat by the shimmering pond, their hearts full of joy. They looked at each other and realized that they hadn't made a wish together yet.

"What should we wish for, Emma?" Sophia asked, her eyes shining with curiosity.

Emma smiled, touched by her friend's question. "I think our friendship is the most precious thing in the world. Let's wish that our friendship remains as magical as this garden forever."

So, they closed their eyes, held hands, and made their wish. They felt a warm breeze encircle them, and they knew their wish had been granted.

Days turned into weeks, and Emma and Sophia continued to visit the enchanted garden, making wishes and sharing adventures. But as time passed, they noticed something remarkable – the wishes they made in the garden weren't the only things coming true.

Their friendship grew stronger with each passing day. They supported each other through life's ups and downs, lending a hand when one needed help, and offering a shoulder to cry on when the other faced challenges. They laughed together, shared their dreams, and cherished every moment they spent in each other's company.

One day, as they sat by the pond, Sophia said, "You know, Emma, this garden is amazing, and our wishes have come true, but I've come to realize that the real magic is in our friendship. It's the laughter, the support, and the love we share that make every day feel like a wish come true."

Emma nodded in agreement, her eyes shimmering with gratitude. "You're absolutely right, Sophia. Our friendship is the most magical thing in the world, and it's a treasure we'll cherish forever."

And so, as Emma and Sophia continued to visit the enchanted garden, they made fewer wishes for themselves because they already had everything they needed – a friendship that was more enchanting and magical than any wish could ever be.

The garden remained their secret place, a reminder of the wonderful adventures they had shared and the countless more they would have. And in the warmth of their friendship, they found the truest and most powerful magic of all.

As they grew older, their bond remained unbreakable, and

they continued to explore the world together, facing life's challenges with the strength of their friendship. And in the end, they knew that the real treasure in life was not the wishes they made but the love and support they gave each other through life's ups and downs.

28

Harper's Goalkeeping Challenge

In a small town nestled between rugged hills and deep forests, there lived a determined young girl named Harper.

Harper was known for her unwavering spirit and boundless enthusiasm, which she poured into her love for soccer. From the moment she could walk, she had been kicking a soccer ball around, dreaming of becoming a goalkeeper.

As Harper grew older, her passion for soccer intensified. She watched every game on television, studied famous goalkeepers, and practiced tirelessly in her backyard.

But there was something that made Harper stand out from the other kids who loved the sport. Harper was petite, much shorter than her peers, and this difference was especially noticeable on the soccer field.

One sunny afternoon, as Harper was playing with her friends at the local park, they noticed a flyer for the town's youth soccer team tryouts. The excitement bubbled up inside her. It was her chance to chase her dreams and prove that her height didn't define her abilities. Without hesitation, she decided to try out for the team.

The day of the tryouts arrived, and Harper stood in line with the other hopefuls. She couldn't help but feel a bit self-conscious about her height as she looked around at the taller, more imposing figures. Nevertheless, she was determined to give it her all.

The tryouts were intense. The coach assessed the players' dribbling, passing, and shooting skills. When it came time for the goalkeeping tryout, Harper's heart raced with both excitement and nervousness. She knew that this was her chance to shine, to prove that she could be a valuable asset to the team.

As the coach sent shots flying her way, Harper dove, jumped, and stretched her small frame to make incredible saves. She exhibited an unmatched determination and agility that caught the coach's attention. When the tryouts concluded, Harper was overjoyed to find her name on the list of players who had made the team. She had become the goalkeeper she had always dreamt of being.

However, not everyone on the team was as supportive as the coach. Some of her teammates, especially a couple of the older boys, couldn't resist making fun of Harper for her height. They called her names and teased her mercilessly, making her feel small in more ways than one.

At first, Harper tried to ignore the bullies and focus on her game. She knew that she belonged on the team, and she wasn't going to let anyone's hurtful words deter her. But as the taunts continued, it became increasingly difficult to maintain her composure.

One day, during a practice session, the teasing reached a breaking point. The bullies were relentless in their efforts to make Harper feel inferior. They even went as far as to mock her every time a goal was scored against her in practice. Harper's eyes welled up with tears, and her love for the game began to waver.

That evening, Harper confided in her parents about the bullying she had been enduring. They listened with empathy, their hearts aching for their brave daughter. Harper's mother, a wise and compassionate woman, shared a story from her own childhood. She had faced similar challenges but had learned a valuable lesson about the power of perseverance.

With newfound determination, Harper decided that she would not let the bullies dictate her happiness or her love for soccer. She approached the coach and asked for extra goalkeeper training sessions to improve her skills. She practiced tirelessly, honing her agility, reflexes, and decision-making.

As Harper continued to work hard, her skills as a goalkeeper improved dramatically. During games, she made remarkable saves that left spectators in awe. Her teammates, who had once doubted her, began to respect her as a crucial member of the team.

One day, during a particularly important game, Harper faced a penalty kick that could determine the outcome. The opposing team's striker, renowned for his accuracy, stepped up to take the shot. Harper took a deep breath, focused all her energy, and made a miraculous save, deflecting the ball just inches from the goalpost. The crowd erupted into cheers, and her teammates rushed to celebrate with her.

In that moment, Harper realized that her height didn't define her abilities, and neither did the bullies' hurtful words. She had found the courage to stand up for herself and prove that being different could be an asset. She had become the brave little goalkeeper who defied expectations and earned the respect and admiration of her teammates and peers.

Harper's story became an inspiration not only to her friends but to anyone who faced challenges and adversity. She showed that with determination, perseverance, and unwavering self-belief, one could overcome any obstacle, no matter how big or small, and achieve greatness on their own terms.

35

Max the Bully

In a quiet suburban neighborhood, there lived a bright and determined girl named Sarah.

She was known for her quick wit, kindness, and an unwavering sense of justice. Sarah had a heart of gold, and she believed in standing up for what was right, no matter the circumstances.

Sarah attended a local elementary school, where she was in the same class as a notorious bully named Max. Max was tall for his age, with a booming voice and a knack for making others feel small. He would often tease, taunt, and belittle his classmates, especially those who were more timid or vulnerable.

Sarah couldn't stand the way Max treated her friends and classmates. She believed that everyone deserved to be treated with kindness and respect. One day, when Max targeted a shy boy named Leo, who had recently joined the class, Sarah decided it was time to take a stand.

During recess, Sarah approached Leo, who was sitting alone on a bench, looking dejected. She introduced herself with a warm smile and struck up a conversation. Leo, grateful for the friendly gesture, began to open up to Sarah.

As they talked, Leo revealed that Max had been relentlessly bullying him since he started attending the school. Sarah's heart sank as she listened to Leo's experiences. She knew she couldn't let this continue.

The next day, Sarah decided to put her plan into action. She had a reputation for being clever and resourceful, and she was determined to use her wits to stand up to Max and protect her classmates. She enlisted the help of her friends, Lily and Ben, who were equally fed up with Max's behavior.

Their plan was simple yet effective. During lunchtime, as Max was surrounded by his friends, Sarah, Lily, and Ben approached him with a proposal. Sarah spoke with a calm but firm voice.

"Max, we want to challenge you to a friendly competition," she began. "We think you're really good at a lot of things, and we'd like to see if you can use your skills for something positive."

Max, intrigued by the challenge, agreed to listen. Sarah explained that they wanted to organize a school-wide talent show to showcase everyone's unique abilities. They believed it would be a great opportunity for Max to demonstrate his leadership and charisma in a positive way.

Max hesitated but eventually agreed to participate. Sarah, Lily, and Ben worked tirelessly to organize the talent show, and Max surprised everyone by using his charisma to encourage his classmates to join in.

As the talent show approached, the entire school buzzed with excitement. Students prepared acts ranging from singing and dancing to magic tricks and storytelling.

Sarah, Lily, and Ben had managed to transform the negative energy surrounding Max into a positive and inclusive event.

On the day of the talent show, the auditorium was filled with eager parents, teachers, and students. Max took the stage as the emcee, charming the audience with his charisma and humor. He introduced each act with enthusiasm and encouraged everyone to support their classmates.

As the show went on, Sarah noticed a remarkable change in Max. He seemed genuinely happy and proud to be part of such a positive event. It was as if he had found a new purpose, one that didn't involve hurting others.

Leo, the shy boy who had been Max's target, performed a beautiful piano piece, earning thunderous applause from the audience. Sarah beamed with pride as she watched her friend shine on stage.

After the talent show, Max approached Sarah with a sheepish smile. "You were right, Sarah," he admitted. "I never realized how much fun it could be to use my talents in a positive way. I'm sorry for the way I treated Leo and others."

Sarah, with her compassionate nature, forgave Max and saw that he was genuinely changing for the better. Max, in turn, apologized to Leo and began to mend his relationships with his classmates. The talent show had not only showcased the students' abilities but also taught Max a valuable lesson about kindness and empathy.

From that day on, Max became a role model for standing up against bullying and using one's strengths for good. Sarah, Lily, and Ben had not only tamed the classroom bully but also turned him into an ally in the fight against cruelty and injustice.

Their story spread throughout the school, inspiring others to stand up for what was right and to use their unique talents to make a positive difference in the lives of others. Sarah's determination and courage had not only protected her classmates but had also shown them the power of unity, compassion, and the importance of standing up for what's right.

Lisa's Heart Locket

In a quaint little town, nestled between rolling hills and a sparkling river, there lived a curious and imaginative girl named Lisa. Lisa had always been known for her insatiable curiosity and her love for exploring the world around her.

She had an infectious enthusiasm for life that drew people to her like a magnet.

One sunny afternoon, as Lisa was playing near the riverbank, her grandmother, Rose, approached with a small, heart-shaped locket in her hand. The locket was delicate, with intricate engravings on its surface, and it had been passed down through generations in their family.

"Lisa," Rose began with a warm smile, "I want you to have this locket. It once belonged to your grandfather, who was a true hero."

Lisa's eyes sparkled with excitement as she accepted the locket from her grandmother's hand.

She opened it gently and found a faded photograph of a handsome young man in a military uniform. Her grandfather had a strong, kind face, and Lisa felt an immediate connection to him, even though she had never met him.

Rose began to share the story of Lisa's grandfather, Michael. He had been a courageous soldier who had fought in a war many years ago, a war that had tested the strength of nations and the hearts of families. As Rose spoke, Lisa hung onto every word, her imagination whisking her away to a time when her grandfather had been a young man full of dreams and determination.

She learned about Michael's sacrifices and the challenges he had faced during his time in the military. He had been far away from his family, separated by war, yet he had never lost hope and had remained steadfast in his love for them.

Lisa was deeply moved by her grandmother's storytelling. She realized that her grandfather's heroism wasn't just a distant tale from the past but a part of her own family history. She admired him for his bravery and the love he had for his family and his country.

Over the weeks that followed, Lisa carried the heart-shaped locket with her everywhere she went. It felt like a precious treasure, a link to her grandfather and the sacrifices he had made for his loved ones. She decided that she wanted to learn more about the war he had fought in and the experiences he had gone through.

She spent hours at the local library, reading books and articles about the war, and she even interviewed her grandmother to gather more stories and memories of her grandfather. With each new piece of information, Lisa's admiration for her grandfather grew stronger.

One evening, while going through some old family letters and photographs, Lisa discovered a heartfelt letter written by her grandfather to her grandmother. It was a love letter filled with longing and affection. In it, Michael expressed his deep feelings for Rose and his yearning to return home to her and their family.

As Lisa read the letter, tears welled up in her eyes. She realized that her grandparents' love had endured through the most challenging of times, separated by war but bound by a love that transcended distance and hardship. It was a love story that had stood the test of time.

Inspired by her grandparents' enduring love and her grandfather's bravery, Lisa decided to create a special project for her school. She wanted to honor not only her grandfather but also all the courageous soldiers who had sacrificed for their country.

With Rose's guidance, Lisa collected stories and photographs of war heroes from their town and created a beautiful display in the local community center.

The exhibit showcased the faces and stories of the brave men and women who had served in the military, reminding everyone of the sacrifices made for the sake of freedom and love of family.

The exhibit became a place of reflection and gratitude for the entire town. Families visited, sharing stories of their own relatives who had served in wars past and present. It became a way for the community to come together, to remember, and to honor the heroes who had given so much.

Lisa's heart-shaped locket, which had once held the photograph of her grandfather, now symbolized the sacrifices of all the heroes who had served their country. It served as a reminder that love and family were worth fighting for, and that the sacrifices of the past should never be forgotten.

As Lisa looked at the heart-shaped locket, she felt a profound sense of gratitude for her grandparents, her family, and all those who had served in the name of love and freedom.

She understood that the locket was not just a piece of jewelry but a symbol of the enduring power of love, sacrifice, and the value of family, and it would forever remind her of the heroes who had touched her life in the most profound way.

The Secret Treasure Chest

They knew the answer was hidden among the carved names. Patiently, they examined the ancient inscriptions until they discovered a tiny silver key that fit one of the keyholes. As the chest unlocked, a soft breeze rustled the willow's leaves, as though nature itself celebrated their discovery.

The third riddle guided them to the town's quaint little library, a place filled with stories and knowledge. The riddle read:

"Within the tomes of knowledge vast, in pages turned from first to last, seek the key where words hold sway, and wisdom lights the darkest day."

They searched the library's shelves until they found an old, leather-bound book with a small bronze key wedged between its pages. With their newfound key, the chest revealed even more of its enchanting treasures.

The fourth and final riddle took them to the highest hill in the town, where a solitary oak tree stood with its branches reaching for the sky. The riddle read:

"High above where dreams take flight, where the oak stands tall and might, find the key within its grasp, to open secrets of the past."

They climbed the hill and discovered a tiny emerald key nestled among the oak's branches. As they inserted it into the last keyhole, a brilliant burst of light radiated from the chest, and its contents began to shimmer and transform.

The girls gathered around as the chest revealed a magnificent, ancient book with gilded pages. It was a book of forgotten tales, filled with stories of courage, friendship, and magic. Each page held a new adventure, and they realized that the riddles had led them to discover the keys to unlock the book's secrets.

With the book in their hands, they returned to Seraphina's backyard, where they gathered in a circle, ready to read the stories within. As they turned the pages, they were transported into magical worlds, where they became brave heroes, wise sorceresses, and daring explorers.

With every story they read, they learned valuable lessons about courage, kindness, and the boundless power of imagination. Each adventure strengthened their friendship, and they realized that their journey to unlock the chest had been a quest not just for treasures but for the magic of shared experiences and cherished memories.

As the sun began to set, the girls closed the ancient book, their hearts filled with gratitude for the extraordinary day they had shared. They knew that the chest, the riddles, and the magical stories would forever remind them of the incredible adventures they could undertake together.

With their bonds of friendship stronger than ever, Seraphina, Elowen, Celestia, and Orla knew that they were truly explorers of the heart, finding treasures far more precious than gold—each other's company and the enchanting stories that would forever connect them to the extraordinary summer day when they unlocked the secrets of the chest.

53

The Lost
Necklace

In the charming town of Brookville, nestled between rolling hills, lived a girl named Tara. Tara was known for her kindness, her radiant smile, and the precious necklace she always wore.

It was a delicate silver chain with a tiny heart-shaped locket, a gift from her father on her birthday. Inside the locket, there was a tiny photograph of the two of them, a symbol of their unbreakable bond.

One sunny morning, as Tara was getting ready for school, she realized with a sinking feeling that her necklace was no longer around her neck. Panic gripped her heart, and she frantically searched her room, her school bag, and even the laundry. But the necklace was nowhere to be found.

Tara's eyes welled up with tears as she realized that she had lost the precious gift from her father. She knew she had to find it, and she couldn't do it alone. She called her friends, Mia, Oliver, and Leo, and explained her predicament.

Without hesitation, her friends rushed to her side. They knew how much the necklace meant to Tara, and they were determined to help her find it. They began their search at school, retracing Tara's steps, checking every classroom, hallway, and nook and cranny.

As the day wore on, they expanded their search to the nearby areas, scouring the park where they played after school and the ice cream shop where they often gathered.

Tara's heart ached with worry, and her friends could see the distress in her eyes.

Days turned into weeks, and despite their relentless efforts, the necklace remained elusive. Tara's friends watched as she went from hopeful to despondent. They knew that the necklace was irreplaceable, but they also understood that their support meant more to Tara than any material possession.

One evening, as Tara sat on a bench in the park, her friends joined her. Mia placed a comforting hand on her shoulder and said, "Tara, we've looked everywhere, but we can't find your necklace. We're really sorry."

Tara nodded, her eyes filled with tears. "I know you tried your best," she said softly. "I just wish I could find it. It meant the world to me because my dad gave it to me before he left for his business trip."

Leo, Oliver, and Mia exchanged glances. They hated seeing Tara so upset, and they wished there was something they could do to make her feel better.

Just as they were about to offer Tara some ice cream to cheer her up, Leo noticed something glinting in the grass beneath the bench. He bent down and picked it up, and to everyone's astonishment, it was Tara's necklace.

Tara's eyes widened, and she gasped in disbelief. "My necklace! How did it end up here?"

Oliver grinned. "It must have fallen off when we were playing tag the other day. It was hiding right under our noses all this time."

Tara hugged her friends tightly, her heart brimming with joy. The necklace was more than just a piece of jewelry; it was a symbol of her father's love, and now, it had become a symbol of the unwavering support and camaraderie of her friends.

As they walked back home, Tara realized that sometimes the most precious   treasures weren't material possessions but the bonds of friendship and the love of family. She knew that her father would be overjoyed to see how her friends had rallied around her during this difficult time.

The necklace now held an even more special place in Tara's heart, and she wore it with a renewed sense of gratitude. She knew that with friends like Mia, Oliver, and Leo by her side, she could overcome any challenge, no matter how daunting.

And so, in the charming town of Brookville, amidst the rolling hills and beside the winding river, Tara learned that sometimes, what is lost can be found in the most unexpected places, and that the true treasures in life were the love and support of the people who cared about you the most.

Jemma's
Determination

In the bustling heart of Willowville City, a spirited and determined girl named Jemma lived with a heart full of dreams and a passion that set her apart from her peers – she loved cycling.

One sunny day, as Jemma was riding her trusty old bike through the city streets, she saw a poster on the school bulletin board. It announced tryouts for the school's cycling team. Her eyes sparkled with excitement. This was her chance to showcase her love for cycling and perhaps become part of something she had always dreamed of.

But as Jemma walked into the city's grand indoor arena on the day of tryouts, she couldn't help but notice the skeptical looks from some of the students. You see, Jemma was not like the other kids who had sleek, modern bicycles. Her bike was a hand-me-down from her older brother, its paint chipped and its tires slightly worn. It wasn't flashy or new, but it carried years of memories and determination.

The coach, Coach Davis, welcomed everyone and explained the tryout process. Jemma's heart pounded with anticipation as she lined up with the other hopefuls. They were given a challenging course to ride, filled with twists, turns, and steep hills. Jemma was determined to show her skills, despite the doubts that hung in the air.

As she pedaled her heart out, her old bike groaned and squeaked, but Jemma's determination propelled her forward. She felt the wind rush through her hair as she conquered the course, and when she crossed the finish line, she couldn't help but wear a triumphant smile.

However, the doubtful expressions from her peers didn't fade away. Coach Davis approached Jemma with a concerned look. "You did well," he said, "but you know, it's a tough competition, and your bike... well, it's not the best."

Jemma nodded, her spirit undeterred. She was determined to prove herself. She knew she had to work even harder to earn a spot on the team.

Every day after school, Jemma would head to the bustling streets of Willowville City with her bike. She practiced tirelessly, pushing herself to the limits. She navigated through traffic, darting between cars with precision. She knew that if she wanted to be a part of the cycling team, she had to be the best.

One evening, while training in a city park, Jemma noticed a group of boys from her school watching her. They had always been skeptical about her abilities, but this time, they seemed genuinely impressed by her dedication and hard work. They even offered her some tips and encouragement.

Days turned into weeks, and Jemma's progress was undeniable. Her dedication paid off when she received a l etter inviting her to compete in a citywide cycling event. It was a chance to prove her skills to everyone, especially to those who doubted her because of her bike and her gender.

The day of the event arrived, and Jemma was filled with a mixture of excitement and nerves. As she lined up at the starting line in the heart of Willowville City, she couldn't help but notice that many of her schoolmates were there to cheer her on. Her heart swelled with gratitude for the support she had received from her friends.

The race was intense, with competitors pushing themselves to the limits through the city's bustling streets. Jemma faced formidable challenges but relied on her training and determination. She pedaled harder, pushed through fatigue, and finally, as she approached the finish line in the heart of the city, she gave it her all.

In a thrilling moment that seemed to pause time itself, Jemma crossed the finish line, triumphant and victorious. The cheers from her friends and the crowd echoed through the bustling city streets. She had not only won the race but also earned the respect and admiration of everyone who had once doubted her.

Jemma's journey had been a testament to her unwavering determination and the power of believing in oneself. She had proven that it didn't matter if her bike was old or if she was a girl in a male-dominated sport. What mattered most was the passion, hard work, and unshakable belief in her abilities.

As Jemma stood there, holding her trophy high in the heart of Willowville City, she knew that she had not only earned a place on the school's cycling team but also earned a newfound sense of self-respect and the respect of her peers.

Her journey had been a thrilling ride against the wind, and it had made her stronger, more determined, and ready to conquer any challenge that lay ahead.

With her friends by her side, Jemma's love for cycling continued to grow, and she knew that there were no limits to what she could achieve. In the bustling heart of Willowville City, she had not only become a skilled cyclist but also a source of inspiration for others who dared to dream big and chase their passions, no matter the odds.

The Neighborhood Dragon

In the peaceful suburban neighborhood of Maple Street, nestled between rows of charming houses and towering maple trees, a captivating rumor had been circulating among the local children. This intriguing tale told of a fierce and mighty dragon dwelling within the confines of Mr. Thompson's garage.

As the sun cast long shadows one bright afternoon, Eliza, a curious and imaginative girl, found herself drawn to the mystery surrounding the mythical creature. While the other children reveled in the excitement of the unknown, Eliza felt an irresistible urge to uncover the truth behind this enigmatic legend.

Summoning her courage, she approached Mr. Thompson's house and knocked on the weathered front door. It creaked open to reveal Mr. Thompson, a tall and gentle man whose eyes held a glimmer of curiosity beneath a wispy white beard.

"Hello there, young lady," Mr. Thompson greeted Eliza, his voice kind and inviting.

"Hi, Mr. Thompson," Eliza replied with determination. "I've been hearing stories about a dragon in your garage. Is it true?"

A warm chuckle escaped Mr. Thompson's lips as he nodded. "Ah, the dragon tale, I see. Come with me; I'll show you."

Eliza followed Mr. Thompson to the garage, her heart racing. As the door slowly ascended, it unveiled the interior, revealing not a terrifying dragon but a massive and friendly dog lounging on a cushion.

Eliza blinked in astonishment. "This is the dragon?"

Mr. Thompson laughed softly. "Indeed, this is Dragon. He's no dragon, just a gentle, lovable dog."

Eliza couldn't help but smile as Dragon thumped his tail and woofed in greeting. The imaginations of the other children had woven a whimsical narrative around this gentle giant.

"Do you want to meet him?" Mr. Thompson asked.

Eliza eagerly nodded, and Mr. Thompson led her into the garage. Dragon's eyes lit up with delight as Eliza approached. She extended her hand, and Dragon nuzzled it affectionately, his eyes brimming with warmth.

"He's the friendliest dragon I've ever met," Eliza remarked, her initial fear dissolving into a deep sense of affection.

Mr. Thompson grinned. "Indeed, he is. I adopted Dragon from the animal shelter a few years ago. He may not be a mythical creature, but his heart is as big as one."

As the days passed, Eliza's newfound friendship with Dragon flourished. She discovered that the dragon legend had been the product of youthful imaginations running wild. In reality, Dragon was a gentle giant who reveled in belly rubs, leisurely walks, and spirited games of fetch.

Her bond with Mr. Thompson also grew stronger as they shared stories and laughter over cups of tea. Eliza learned about the quirks and characteristics of dogs, gaining insight into their various breeds and unique behaviors. She gladly assisted Mr. Thompson with Dragon's care, whether it was brushing his fur or indulging him with tasty treats.

News of Eliza's discovery gradually spread throughout the neighborhood, and soon, other children were just as amazed as she had been. They, too, paid visits to Mr. Thompson's garage, and before long, Dragon had an enthusiastic group of young admirers.

As the seasons transitioned from summer to autumn, and the maple trees donned their vibrant fall colors, Eliza reflected on her experience. She realized that truth could often be more captivating than fiction. Her initial apprehension of the dragon had transformed into deep affection for the lovable giant, and she had also gained a profound understanding of the power of imagination and the strength of community bonds.

In the tranquil neighborhood of Maple Street, where the line between reality and legend blurred, Eliza, Mr. Thompson, and Dragon shared a unique and enduring connection. It served as a heartwarming reminder that friendship could be discovered in the most unexpected places, even within the depths of a dragon's lair.

The tale of Dragon the dog and the dragon's lair on Maple Street became a cherished part of the neighborhood's lore. Children from far and wide came to visit and hear the story of the gentle dragon who had won over the hearts of everyone in the community. Mr. Thompson's garage became a gathering place for laughter and play, where the

boundaries of fantasy and reality merged seamlessly.

As the winter snow blanketed Maple Street in a soft, white embrace, Eliza, Mr. Thompson, and Dragon continued their adventures together.

They embarked on snowy hikes and built intricate snow forts in the yard, Dragon's fluffy tail wagging all the while. The bond between them grew stronger with each passing day, a testament to the magic of friendship and the warmth it brought even in the coldest of seasons.

The heartwarming tale of the Maple Street dragon became a symbol of unity and kindness within the neighborhood. It was a reminder that, sometimes, the most extraordinary stories could be found in the ordinary corners of our lives. The children of Maple Street learned the valuable lesson that the power of imagination and the beauty of genuine connections could transform a simple garage into a sanctuary of wonder and joy.

In the years that followed, the legend of Dragon lived on, passed down from one generation of Maple Street children to the next.

Dragon may not have been a fire-breathing dragon from the pages of a storybook, but he was something even more extraordinary – a source of love and companionship that touched the hearts of all who crossed his path.

And so, in the peaceful suburban neighborhood of Maple Street, nestled between rows of charming houses and towering maple trees, the legend of the dragon in Mr. Thompson's garage continued to thrive. It was a story that celebrated the boundless imagination of youth, the enduring bonds of friendship, and the enchanting magic that could be found in the most unexpected places.

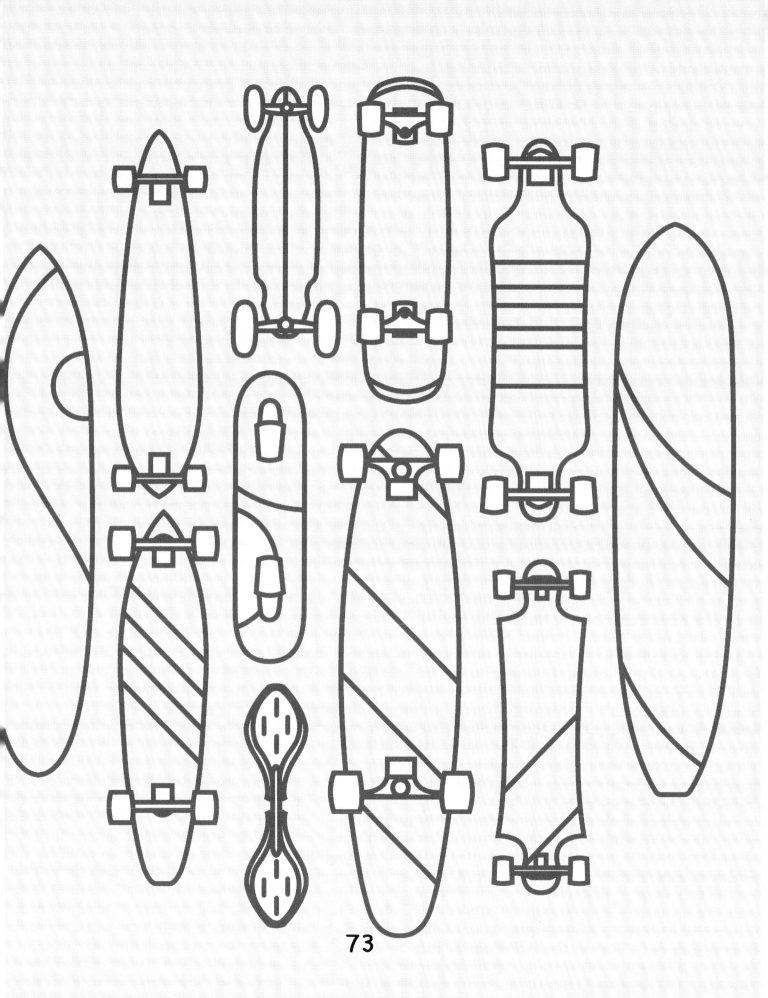

Skating is For Girls

Amidst the rhythmic clatter of wheels on concrete, in the heart of their neighborhood, there was a vibrant skate park where the local kids congregated daily.

This concrete oasis served as a playground for those who had mastered the art of skateboarding, a place where the cool kids reigned supreme with their gravity-defying tricks and fearless attitudes. Among the spectators who often lingered on the park's edge was Jess, a young girl with dreams as big as the sky but a self-doubt that kept her on the sidelines.

Jess admired the skateboarders who soared through the air, executing flips, twists, and daring stunts. The way they effortlessly conquered the ramps and rails fascinated her. She yearned to be part of their world, to experience the exhilaration of gliding through this makeshift arena, but there was a nagging voice inside her that held her back — the voice of insecurity.

She watched her brother, Max, a skilled skateboarder in his own right, weave his way through the crowd of daredevils. He was her idol, the embodiment of coolness, and her hero when it came to all things skateboarding.

Max's effortless grace on his skateboard left her in awe, but it also made her feel small and insignificant. She thought she could never be as cool or skilled as him, and that belief had kept her from ever stepping foot on a skateboard herself.

One sunny afternoon, as the clinks and clatters of the skate park reached a crescendo, Jess made a spontaneous decision. She decided to step out of her comfort zone and confront her fears head-on.

With her heart pounding, she sneaked into her brother's room and borrowed his old skateboard. It was worn and scratched, a testament to Max's countless hours of practice and adventure. Jess hesitated for a moment, but her desire

to break free from her insecurities was stronger.

She rolled the skateboard out onto the driveway, the wheels spinning hesitantly at first. Jess took a deep breath, her hands trembling as they touched the rough grip tape on the deck. With a shaky push of her foot, she started moving, wobbling as she struggled to find her balance. The feeling of vulnerability was overwhelming, and she fell onto the pavement with a thud.

For days, Jess practiced in secret. She ventured out early in the morning or late at night when the park was empty, away from the judging eyes of the seasoned skateboarders. Bruised knees, scraped elbows, and countless falls became her companions on this journey. But Jess was determined, and with each tumble, she picked herself up, dusted off her doubts, and pushed forward.

Weeks turned into months, and Jess's secret practice sessions began to yield progress. She gradually gained confidence, learning to balance and maneuver on the skateboard with more finesse. Her wobbles turned into controlled glides, and she started attempting simple tricks. Still, she kept her newfound passion hidden from everyone, including Max.

One sunny afternoon, Max caught Jess in the act. He had returned home early from the skate park and discovered her practicing in the driveway. His eyes widened in surprise as he watched his little sister skateboarding with determination and grit. Instead of laughing or scolding her for using his old board, Max smiled and offered his support.

"Hey, Jess," Max said, "want me to show you a few tricks?"

Jess, initially embarrassed by her secret being exposed, now felt a surge of pride. Her brother, her idol, was offering to teach her. She nodded eagerly, and together, they spent hours perfecting her moves. Max's encouragement and guidance were invaluable, and Jess realized that she didn't need to be exactly like him to be cool.

As the days passed, Jess continued to practice, now with her brother and sometimes even other skaters from the park. Her skills improved, and she started to join the other kids at the skatepark. At first, she was nervous, feeling like an outsider among the cool crowd. But as she demonstrated her newfound abilities, the skaters welcomed her with open arms.

Jess had discovered that being herself was the coolest thing of all. She didn't have to be a replica of her brother or anyone else. Her unique style and determination made her stand out in the skateboarding world, and her friends at the park admired her for it.

Jess had not only conquered her fear of skateboarding but also her fear of being different. She had learned that true coolness came from within, from being authentic and embracing one's individuality.

The skate park, once a place of intimidation and self-doubt, had become Jess's second home. She had found her passion, her confidence, and a group of friends who appreciated her for who she was.

As she glided through the concrete arena, executing tricks with grace and enthusiasm, Jess knew that she had not only become a skateboarder but also a star in her own right. And she owed it all to the courage it took to be herself.

Messages on the Sidewalk

Lauren, a spirited seven-year-old living in a bustling neighborhood, had a penchant for creating colorful chalk art on the sidewalk outside her apartment building.

This creative pursuit became a cherished part of her daily routine, filling the pavement with her imaginative drawings. But one sunny day, she decided to add a little something extra to her sidewalk masterpieces that would touch the hearts of her neighbors and remind them of the power of love and positivity.

With her sidewalk chalk in hand, Lauren embarked on her artistic endeavor. She carefully wrote the word "Smile" next to her radiant sun drawing, using pink chalk. It was a simple message, but it carried the warmth and optimism that flowed from her heart.

Lauren stood back, admiring her work with a wide smile. She had a simple hope – that someone passing by might see her message and, even if just for a moment, feel a little brighter. What she didn't realize was the profound impact her small act of kindness was about to have on her neighborhood.

The next morning, Lauren's mom, Emily, glanced out of their apartment window and noticed something remarkable. A group of neighbors, including Mr. Johnson, the elderly gentleman from the third floor, and Sarah, the single mom with two young children, were gathered around Lauren's sidewalk art. They were smiling and laughing, their faces filled with newfound cheer.

Curious, Emily made her way downstairs to join the group. Mr. Johnson greeted her with a twinkle in his eye. "Have you seen what your daughter's been up to, Emily?" he asked.

Emily shook her head, intrigued by the scene before her. She approached the vibrant chalk drawings and read the message, "Smile," next to the sun. A warm feeling washed over her as she realized what Lauren had done.

Over the next few days, Lauren continued her sidewalk chalk messages. Each day, she'd leave a new drawing accompanied by an uplifting message. "You're Awesome" next to a whimsical rainbow, "Shine Bright" next to a radiant star, and "Be Kind" alongside a picture of a heart. Her messages of love and encouragement transformed the sidewalk into an ever-changing gallery of positivity.

As the days turned into weeks, the neighborhood began to buzz with excitement over Lauren's daily surprises. The messages served as gentle reminders to embrace the simple joys of life, to be kind to one another, and to cherish the beauty of the present moment.

Sarah, the single mom, confided in Emily one afternoon, "Those messages from Lauren have turned my kids' walks to school into moments of joy. They look forward to seeing what new message she's left for them each day."

Mr. Johnson, who had lived in the neighborhood for decades,

shared, "I've seen a lot in my time, but I've never seen anything quite like this. It's like a ray of sunshine every morning."

Lauren's messages began to have a ripple effect throughout the neighborhood. People started smiling more, striking up conversations with their neighbors, and performing small acts of kindness for one another. The sense of community and connection deepened as a result of a little girl's heartfelt expressions of love and positivity.

One day, as Lauren finished drawing a bright rainbow with the message "Spread Love," a neighbor named Mrs. Miller approached her. She had tears in her eyes as she said, "Lauren, your messages have been such a blessing. They've been a source of comfort during difficult times."

Lauren hugged Mrs. Miller tightly, her heart swelling with happiness. It was a moment that crystallized the profound impact of her small acts of love.

As the weeks turned into months, Lauren's chalk messages became an integral part of the neighborhood's daily routine.

People looked forward to the surprises she left on the sidewalk, and the sense of community grew stronger than ever. What started as a simple act of kindness from a seven-year-old girl had blossomed into a powerful reminder that love and positivity could make a significant difference, even in the most unexpected places.

Lauren had not just brightened the neighborhood's sidewalks; she had illuminated their hearts and souls, leaving an indelible mark on their lives. And in the process, she learned a valuable lesson – that even small acts of love and kindness could create a ripple effect of joy and togetherness that extended far beyond the pavement.

But Lauren wasn't done yet. She wanted to continue spreading love and positivity in her neighborhood, and her creativity knew no bounds. With each passing day, her chalk art became more elaborate, and her messages more heartwarming.

One sunny afternoon, Lauren decided to draw a magnificent tree with vibrant leaves of all colors. She added the message "Grow Strong" next to it. As she finished her artwork, she noticed a mother and her daughter watching from a distance. The little girl, about her age, had a somber expression.

Lauren approached them and said, "Hi! I'm Lauren. Do you like my drawing?"

The girl smiled shyly and nodded. "I'm Emma. Your drawing is beautiful."

Lauren then asked, "Would you like to draw with me? We can create something amazing together."

Emma's eyes lit up with excitement as she eagerly accepted the offer. The two girls spent the afternoon drawing and chatting, their laughter filling the air. By the end of the day, they had created a masterpiece that was not only visually stunning but also a symbol of the new friendship they had forged.

As the weeks went by, Lauren and Emma became inseparable friends. They continued to spread love and positivity through their sidewalk chalk art, now a dynamic duo inspiring the entire neighborhood. Their messages of kindness, encouragement, and unity brought people together like never before.

One sunny weekend, Lauren organized a sidewalk art event for the entire neighborhood. She invited everyone to come and create their own chalk masterpieces, encouraging them to express their feelings, hopes, and dreams. It turned into a festive gathering, with neighbors of all ages participating.

Neighbors like Mr. Johnson and Sarah drew pictures of their own, adding their unique touch to the colorful sidewalk canvas. Even Mrs. Miller, who had been going through a difficult time, created a heartfelt message of gratitude and hope.

As the day came to a close, the entire sidewalk was covered with beautiful chalk art, and the messages of love and positivity stretched as far as the eye could see. The neighborhood had been transformed into a vibrant, living work of art.

Lauren's mom, Emily, was overwhelmed by the sense of

community and togetherness that had blossomed in their neighborhood.

She approached her daughter and said, "Lauren, you've brought so much joy and unity to our neighborhood with your chalk art and kindness. You've shown us that even the smallest gestures of love can make a big difference."

Lauren beamed with pride, knowing that her actions had not only brightened the lives of those around her but also strengthened the bonds within her community. She had discovered the incredible power of spreading love, positivity, and kindness.

88

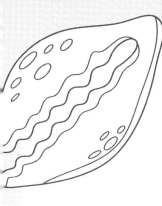

Searching for Seashells

Beth was a young girl with a heart full of wonder and a love for collecting seashells. Every weekend, she would visit the local beach, where the rhythm of the waves and the salty breeze filled her with a sense of calm.

While many kids her age were into flashy toys or sports, Beth found solace in the art of beachcombing.

With a small bucket in hand and her eyes scanning the shoreline, Beth scoured the sand for the treasures the ocean left behind. She cherished the beauty of each seashell, no matter how small or simple. To her, there was something magical about the way the sea transformed ordinary bits of shell into tiny masterpieces.

Beth's collection grew steadily over the years, and each shell she picked up held a special place in her heart.

However, her classmates at school couldn't quite understand her passion. They teased her for her "boring" hobby and questioned why she didn't spend her time on something more exciting.

One sunny afternoon, as Beth combed the beach, she noticed a group of kids from her school playing beach volleyball. They laughed, shouted, and cheered each other on as they smacked the ball over the net. Beth watched them from a distance, feeling a pang of loneliness. She longed to join in their fun, but she also knew that her heart belonged to the seashells.

As she continued her search, her eyes caught a glimmer of something unusual. Half buried in the sand was a seashell that looked remarkably like a heart. It was as if the ocean itself had sculpted this shell as a special gift just for her. She carefully picked it up, cradling it in her hand, and felt a surge of happiness.

Beth realized that this heart-shaped seashell symbolized more than just a unique find; it represented her love for beachcombing and her ability to see beauty in the smallest things. She decided to carry it with her as a reminder of the magic she found in the ordinary.

With her newfound determination, Beth returned to school on Monday, proudly carrying the heart-shaped seashell in her pocket. When her classmates once again teased her about her "boring" hobby, Beth decided to speak from her heart.

"I know collecting seashells might seem boring to some of you," she began, "but to me, it's a way of finding beauty in the world around us. Each shell I find is like a tiny piece of art created by nature. And you know what? It makes me happy."

Beth's sincerity touched the hearts of her classmates, and the teasing stopped. They may not have shared her passion, but they respected her for being true to herself. Some even began to see the beauty in her collection and started asking her about the different types of shells she had found.

Over time, Beth's classmates realized that her hobby was more than just picking up seashells; it was a way of appreciating the small, often overlooked wonders of the world. Beth's collection became a source of inspiration, reminding them to find joy in simple things and to embrace their own unique interests and passions.

One day, after school, Beth decided to share her collection with her classmates. She organized a "Seashell Showcase" in her backyard, setting up a table with her most prized shells on display. Her classmates were amazed by the variety of shapes, colors, and patterns in her collection. They listened with awe as Beth explained the stories behind each shell and how she had found them.

As the sun began to set, Beth's classmates left her backyard with a newfound appreciation for her hobby. They realized that what made Beth special was not the seashells themselves but her ability to find beauty and meaning in something as simple as a seashell.

Beth's heart-shaped seashell, which had once been a symbol of her love for beachcombing, now symbolized something even more profound — the importance of staying true to oneself and finding joy in the things that made each person unique. It was a lesson in friendship and acceptance, showing that differences could be celebrated rather than ridiculed.

In the end, Beth's love for seashells not only enriched her own life but also touched the lives of those around her. She had shown her classmates that even the seemingly ordinary could hold extraordinary beauty and meaning if viewed with an open heart and a sense of wonder.

As the years passed, Beth's love for beachcombing remained a cherished part of her life. She continued to collect seashells, each one a reminder of the lesson she had learned as a young girl on that sunny day at the beach. And whenever she felt the need to remind herself of the beauty in the world, all she had to do was reach into her pocket and feel the heart-shaped seashell, a constant reminder that the most meaningful treasures were often found in the simplest of places.

94

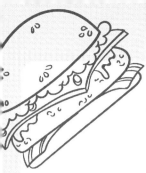

The Art of Giving

Zainab was a young girl with a heart full of compassion and a desire to make a difference in her community.

She lived in a quiet neighborhood where everyone knew one another, and she admired the local firefighters who worked tirelessly to keep her town safe. One sunny afternoon, as she was reading a story about heroes in her favorite book, Zainab stumbled upon a flyer in the community center that piqued her interest.

The flyer announced a charity event being held at the local fire station to raise funds for a new rescue equipment. It was called "Firefighters' Appreciation Day," and it invited the community to come together and show their support. Zainab's eyes lit up with excitement as she read the details. She knew she had to be a part of this event, and she had a special idea in mind.

With determination, Zainab rushed home to her mother, who was busy in the kitchen. "Mom," she exclaimed, "I want to bake cookies for the firefighters for their charity event!"

Her mother smiled warmly and replied, "That's a wonder-ful idea, Zainab. I'll help you make the best cookies they've ever tasted."

Together, they spent the evening mixing ingredients, rolling out dough, and filling their home with the sweet aroma of freshly baked cookies. Zainab carefully shaped the cookies into little fire helmets and fire trucks, adding a personal touch to her heartfelt gift.

The following day, Zainab proudly carried a tray of her homemade cookies to the local fire station. Her heart raced with anticipation as she approached the station's front door. She rang the bell, and a friendly firefighter named Captain Rodriguez opened the door with a warm smile.

"Hello there," Captain Rodriguez greeted her. "How can we help you today?"

Zainab shyly held out the tray of cookies. "I baked these for the charity event. I wanted to say thank you for all that you do."

Captain Rodriguez's eyes twinkled with appreciation as he accepted the tray. "Thank you, Zainab. This is incredibly kind of you. Would you like to come inside and meet the rest of the firefighters?"

Zainab's heart leaped with excitement as she followed Captain Rodriguez inside the fire station. The smell of polished metal and the sound of the station's alarm system filled the air. She felt like she had entered a world of heroes.

The firefighters were delighted by Zainab's gift, and they invited her to stay for the charity event. Zainab gladly accepted the invitation and watched as the community gathered to show their support. There were games for children, food stalls, and even a demonstration of how the fire equipment worked.

As the day went on, Zainab couldn't help but feel a growing sense of connection with the firefighters and the community. She met Firefighter Maya, who showed her the impressive array of firefighting gear they used to keep everyone safe. Zainab was particularly fascinated by the towering fire truck parked in the station.

Seeing her excitement, Captain Rodriguez asked, "Would you like to sit in the fire truck, Zainab?"

Her eyes lit up with joy as she nodded vigorously. With Captain Rodriguez's help, she climbed into the fire truck's cab and gripped the steering wheel, pretending to be a firefighter on a mission. She couldn't stop smiling as the firefighters shared stories of their adventures and the important role they played in the community.

As the charity event drew to a close, Zainab felt a deep sense of fulfillment. She had not only expressed her gratitude to the firefighters but had also experienced firsthand the camaraderie and warmth of her community. She realized that acts of kindness and love could be rewarding in unexpected ways, bringing people closer together and creating lasting memories.

As she prepared to leave the fire station, Captain Rodriguez gave her a small fire department patch as a token of their appreciation. Zainab pinned it to her jacket with pride, knowing that it would remind her of the incredible day she had shared with the local heroes.

Back at home, Zainab couldn't wait to tell her family all about her adventure. She shared stories of the brave firefighters, the exciting tour of the fire station, and the joy of sitting in the fire truck. She also told them about the valuable lesson she had learned – that acts of kindness and love could make a significant impact on others and create a sense of unity within a community.

In the days that followed, Zainab continued to cherish her connection with the local fire station and the firefighters who selflessly served her community. She knew that her simple act of baking cookies had not only brightened their day but had also brought them all closer together.

As Zainab looked out the window at the fire station down the street, she smiled, knowing that her heart was forever linked with the brave firefighters who risked their lives to keep their neighborhood safe.

She had learned that sometimes, the most rewarding gifts were the ones that came from the heart, and that love and appreciation could create bonds that would last a lifetime.

Disclaimer

The book "GIRLS ARE AMAZING: Inspirational and Exciting Short Stories for Girls about Love, Self-Awareness, and Courage" is a work of fiction and is intended solely for entertainment, inspiration, and motivational purposes. While the stories contained within this book are designed to empower and encourage young girls, readers are advised to exercise discretion and judgment when interpreting and applying the themes and messages presented.

The characters and situations depicted in the stories are products of the author's imagination and do not necessarily reflect real-life experiences or events. Any resemblance to actual persons, living or deceased, or to real-life situations is purely coincidental.

The content of this book is not intended to provide professional or medical advice, and readers should consult with appropriate professionals when seeking guidance on specific matters. Additionally, the book does not endorse or promote any particular religious, political, or cultural beliefs, and readers are encouraged to form their own opinions and perspectives.

The author and publisher of "GIRLS ARE AMAZING" disclaim any responsibility for any actions, decisions, or consequences resulting from the use or interpretation of the book's content. Readers are encouraged to use their discretion and judgment in applying the lessons and principles contained herein to their own lives.

Finally, this book is dedicated to inspiring and uplifting young girls, promoting self-awareness and courage, and fostering a sense of love and self-worth. It is our hope that readers find motivation and empowerment within its pages.

Please enjoy "GIRLS ARE AMAZING" responsibly and remember that every girl is indeed amazing in her own unique way.

Printed in Great Britain
by Amazon